Other books by A. K. Yearling

Daring Do and the Quest for the Sapphire Stone

Daring Do and the Griffon's Goblet

Daring Do and the Abyss of Despair

Daring Do and the Razor of Dreams

Daring Do and the Ring of Destiny

Daring Do and the Trek to the Terrifying Tower

Daring Do and the Volcano of Destiny

Daring Do and the Marked Thief of Marapore

Daring Do and the Eternal Flower

Daring Do and the Forbidden City of Clouds

Other books by G. M. Berrow

Twilight Sparkle and the Crystal Heart Spell

Pinkie Pie and the Rockin' Ponypalooza Party!

Rainbow Dash and the Daring Do Double Dare

Rarity and the Curious Case of Charity

Applejack and the Honest-to-Goodness Switcheroo

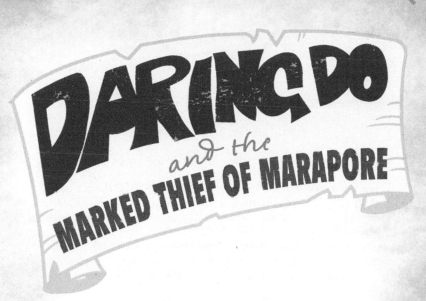

By A. K. Yearling
with G. M. Berrow

Little, Brown and Company
New York Boston

Cover illustration by Franco Spagnolo

Little, Brown and Company

Hachette Book Group
1290 Avenue of the Americas, New York, NY 10104
Visit us at lb-kids.com

Little, Brown and Company is a division of Hachette Book Group, Inc. The Little, Brown name and logo are trademarks of Hachette Book Group, Inc.

The publisher is not responsible for websites (or their content) that are not owned by the publisher.

First Stand-Alone Edition: January 2016
Originally published as part of *My Little Pony: The Daring Do Adventure Collection* in October 2014 by Little, Brown and Company

Library of Congress Control Number: 2014940994

ISBN 978-0-316-30187-9

10 9 8 7 6 5 4 3 2 1

RRD-C

Printed in the United States of America

For my grandmares—
Eunice, Floy, and Rita.
The best things come in threes.

TABLE OF CONTENTS

PROLOGUE

The colossal silver Unicorn glanced back at his mud-smeared flank and cringed. The dirt didn't cover his hideous scar entirely, but hopefully the blanket of the midnight darkness would dim the monstrosity.

"GRRRRRRAW!" He growled in anger,

pacing the steep edge of a vast fiery pit. "Let them see my scar." The pony hung his head in shame as a familiar mix of regret and longing overtook him. It seemed like eons since the incident, yet there he was, back in the very villages he had once sworn to protect. Except this time, he would destroy them.

It was true that without his cutie mark, the stallion had become a mere shadow of his former self. For where there was once joy, there was now endless melancholy. Resentment had replaced kindness, and deep in his heart, cowardice took up residence instead of valor. But the worst part of all was that the inimitable magic that had made him so special in the first place had been damaged beyond repair.

Or so he had thought before learning of the Vehoovius Hex. All it required were a few small sacrifices: some ancient relics, a captive audience, and a little golden pony. Relatively nothing when one considered the reward.

If the hex succeeded, the silver stallion would gain everything back and more. He might even become the most powerful Unicorn in Equestria! He smiled deviously, thinking of all the ways he might use his newfound power. Things were finally looking up now that he had a plan.

He stole one last look at himself in the reflection of a large glass vial. Between his unruly green-and-black mane, bloodshot eyes, and the scar on his flank, he was unrecognizable. What would the villagers think of their celebrated hero now?

"That statue in the center of town should be destroyed. The Stalwart Stallion of Neighples..." The pony sneered as he strode back and forth, watching the molten lava bubble up and fold over into sizzling creases. "Such a *venerated* champion. It makes me sick!" He tore off a piece of a rusty steel bridle lying nearby and tossed it into the fiery goop. Satisfaction surged through his veins as the metal turned a glowing red and melted into an unrecognizable blob. It sank under the liquid and disappeared, never to be seen again. All that was left was the rising steam.

It was time.

The stallion took one last look at his

lair and took off in a canter up a narrow dirt tunnel, his mane and tail billowing behind him. Tonight, he would strike again to get closer to his prize. And there was nopony in all of Equestria who could stop him.

CHAPTER 1

On the High Seas

As Daring Do riffled through her saddle-bag, she began to feel queasy. And it wasn't from the rocking of the great ship upon the choppy, churning sea. It was from the realization that all that was left of her rations—which had once been a carefully selected bounty of dried apples, salted carrots, and seed-crusted loaf—was one stale piece of bread. It wasn't enough to feed a filly.

If only her supplies hadn't been depleted during the storm over the Fillyppine Sea, Daring could have held out longer here on board the SS *Blue Peter*. But a life on the water was an unpredictable one, and the currents had thrown the ship far off course. As a result, the adventurer hadn't been able to sneak off board at any port, let alone into a general store to replenish her provisions. The entire crew was starting to run low on necessary supplies.

Of course, borrowing from the ship's galley again was always an option. But that endeavor would be risky. The sailors took careful inventory of their commodities, and if something went missing, Daring Do would soon be discovered. Three days prior, she'd given into temptation and pilfered a potpie from a tall stack about to be served to the crew for supper. Nopony had noticed. Daring had bitten into the flaky, buttery crust and gooey center with satisfaction.

But later that evening, when she was full-bellied and poring over her tattered map of Deep Unknown—a rare guide to the Submerged Temples of Tehuti—Daring Do overheard the cook, Greasy Spoon, chiding his helper, Square Meal, for eating more than his fair share. Greasy had threatened Square that if he didn't fess up, he'd go without meals for the entirety of the next week. Square Meal lied out of sheer desperation and said he'd eaten two pies, chalking it up to Greasy's amazing cooking skills. That seemed to satisfy his boss.

Daring had felt dreadful for the poor colt during the whole episode, but there was no chance she was going to reveal herself now. Daring had heard many a tall tale in seaside cafés of the consequences for stowing away on Captain Pony the Elder's ship, but they were not something she wished to confirm or deny. Although the captain was no pirate, the military stallion had a reputation for treating stowaways worse than Hoofbeard.

Suddenly, the ship lurched. Dirty pots piled in the washbasin clanked against one another, and Greasy Spoon hollered a curse. Daring's already weakened body slammed against the splintered wooden door, squashing her right wing. She groaned in agony. That wing had never been the same since her nasty crash landing in the jungle near the Yucatán Ponynsula. It vexed her morc than anything to have an injury.

"Grrrr." Daring gritted her teeth as she inspected the aching appendage. It hurt like mad. Maybe she didn't want to admit it to herself, but Daring Do was becoming fatigued by her many weeks at sea in search of the Crystal Sphere of Khumn. Legend said that the magical item could be found in one of the Submerged Temples of Tehuti, located one hundred fathoms below the surface, held by a statue between two golden hooves, beneath a shining metal rod. It was believed that the Sphere had the power to heal anypony who touched it, no matter the ailment. Too bad the fabled ancient city was even harder to find than the Gallopinghost Islands! Like with most treasures, Daring Do felt an intense hunger to find it and make it hers. Or at the very least, stop it from falling into the wrong hooves or claws.

Though she'd been unsuccessful in her quest thus far, she wasn't giving up forever. Daring just needed to do more research, delving deeper into the murky mysteries of Tehuti and Khumn. Then she'd immediately set out on the open seas again. Next time, with more provisions—maybe even dried peppered pears, a few apple tarts, and a small pillow.

A strong gust of cold air blew into the cabin closet where she was crammed. The rickety old mahogany had splintered off in areas, leaving several gaping holes. It was perfect for spying on Captain Pony and his seafaring ruffians (known as the Royal Navy) on board the *Blue Peter*. Not quite ideal for warmth on the high seas, though.

Daring massaged her tender wing. The high winds on board had been rough— too strong for flying. Even so, Daring would never have risked being seen. Not for just a little stretch. She'd surely have been dumped at the nearest port, which was hundreds of miles away from home.

By keeping out of sight, Daring had made it all the way to her destination in one piece.

She thought of her warm bed back in her little cottage in the woods. Daring racked her brain, but she couldn't remember the last time she'd slept there. Before she'd taken off to find the Crystal Sphere of Khumn, she'd been busy searching for the Talisman of Tenochtitlan. And before that, she was waylaid in the jungle with the injured wing, hunting for Ahuizotl's temple. Things never seemed to slow down for Daring Do, but that was the way she preferred it. As far as she was concerned, an idle life was a boring life. There were always treasures to discover and ponies in distress to rescue!

The boatswain, a strong yellow stallion known as Steel Anchor, passed by the tiny porthole in the door of Daring's hideout. She could tell it was Steel by the way his hooves clunked heavily against the ship's wooden deck planks. In fact, Daring could recognize most of the crew now just from weeks of eavesdropping and paying close attention to their little quirks.

"Hey!" Steel Anchor stopped just outside the closet porthole. "Did you hear about old Mo? He *turned*…"

"That so? Darn shame…" added Sea Storm, a junior deck cadet. The pony lowered his voice to a murmur. Daring pressed her ear against the glass so she didn't miss a word. She wasn't sure who Mo was and what he had turned to, but information was precious—no matter what it was. It sounded like the faint glimmer of something intriguing. Sea Storm continued on, "Always had it in 'im, though. Poor chap had been through a lot with his flank situation and all. Nasty thing. Too bad he couldn't—"

But the conversation was abruptly halted by the call of "Land ho!" It was soon followed by another series of shouts from the rest of the crew, bustling around getting the ship ready to dock. They had finally reached port.

"About time," Daring grumbled to herself. She tossed her map, piece of stale bread, and a stolen flagon of cider into her bag and prepared to disembark. If Daring's calculations were correct, the *Blue*

Peter was currently docked at Horseshoe Bay, a sparkling little sapphire inlet on the east coast of Greater Equestria. Once she had successfully escaped the boat, the journey would take about a day to get home—as the Pegasus flies. The thought of stretching her wings made her feathers itch with anticipation.

It was always strange to walk on land after so much time at sea. But at least she had other options. It was going to be wonderful to be on solid ground again, even if it meant that every step she took was going to make Daring's hooves feel like lead. *Ouch!* she mouthed silently as she tried in vain to stretch her wings. The massage hadn't really helped. Apparently, even flying was going to be a struggle.

Here goes nothing, she thought, and hoped for the best. She tore out of the galley, leaped off the ship, and flew as fast as she could into the chilly azure sky. All but one of the crew was too busy to notice her.

Square Meal, the cook's scrawny assistant, stood dumbfounded, scratching his mane, as the stowaway Pegasus became a tiny speck in the distance. Had he really just seen a gold pony with a gray-and-black mane fly out of the kitchen closet? Square Meal then remembered the missing pie and frowned.

"Playtime's over, Captain Pony!" Daring laughed as the ship became increasingly tiny beneath her, its little sails rolling up like the whole craft was about to be stashed in a filly's wooden toy box next to the blocks and dolls. "Thanks for the free ride!" Daring called out with a tip of her pith helmet, though the seafarer didn't hear it. She was already well out of earshot, swooping through gusts and breezes, feeling as free as a dragon during its first migration season.

Even though she was starving, exhausted, and sore, the golden pony couldn't help but smile as she veered her course homeward. She let the fresh, salty air fill her lungs and thought about what would happen next. Whatever it was, Daring Do couldn't wait to figure it out. There was no time for anything else when adventure was calling your name.

CHAPTER 2

A Cloaked Stranger

When Daring Do finally arrived in the woods the next day, she saw somepony pacing back and forth in front of her humble abode. The tiny two-story cottage had a yellow thatched roof and a little brown polka-dot chimney. It wasn't much, but it was home. For the few days a year she wasn't out searching for lost treasures and stolen amulets, at least. The main reason Daring Do liked the place was because it was unassuming—nopony would ever guess that a world-renowned treasure hunter lived there. Nopony, apparently, except *this* stallion.

The golden Pegasus scurried behind a nearby rock, narrowly avoiding the visitor's attention. She'd had enough experience to know that a random pony was not always a good sign. It could be sinister, some sort of trap. Naturally, Daring wasn't afraid of traps, but observing a situation first gave her the upper hoof. "Watch and learn," she always used to tell A. B. Ravenhoof. "Ponies give away more information about themselves just by existing than you could ever pry out of them."

The cloaked pony knocked on the door again, this time a little louder. He was getting impatient. The stallion pushed his green velvet hood back to reveal an unruly golden mane, deep-set eyes, and broad features. His yellow coat was so grimy, he looked like he'd crawled through a gopher tunnel to get there. Clumps of mud and leaves clung to his mane. He smelled strongly of sweet peppered pears, which was incongruous with his dirty, rumpled appearance. He frowned and trotted over to one of the front windows.

Daring Do craned to see his cutie mark. If she could catch a glimpse, maybe she could identify him as either friend or foe. Luckily, his green cloak kept bunching up and sliding into the arch of his back. When the velvet finally cleared away from his flank, Daring saw that the mark was shaped like a yellow rectangle, with black marks along one side. It was a ruler, the kind used in a classroom. Considering Daring Do's photographic memory for cutie marks, she knew instantly that she had never laid eyes on this pony before. Which made him a wild card, a potential loose cannon. Not to be trusted—only to be observed.

Maybe he was one of Dr. Caballeron's lackeys. The jilted Caballeron had never quite gotten over Daring's refusal to work with him as a team, searching for ancient relics and keeping all realms of Equestria safe from the evil designs of the gargantuan blue dog monster Ahuizotl. Now

Caballeron took every chance he got to throw obstacles in Daring's path. If there was something Daring Do was searching for, it was guaranteed that Caballeron would be two trots behind her, picking up the clues left in her wake and trying to make sense of it all so he could take the prize for himself. He needed her, but the feeling was not mutual. Daring Do worked alone—except under extremely rare circumstances. The Rings of Scorchero were proof that much was true.

But who was this mysterious, bedraggled stranger standing in front of her secret woodland cottage? His odd clothing and distinct, foreign features implied that he had traveled quite a distance to find her.

Daring Do recalled meeting a group of ponies with similar-style cloaks on a journey to the Tenochtitlan Basin in the southern latitudes. Daring Do had been en route for weeks, on her way to ransack the camp of the Ketztwctl Empress, hoping to stop her dark magic from ever controlling the Amulet of Atonement again. However, the landmark Daring had chosen happened to be a wandering tree, and she had unwittingly been traveling farther from her destination every day! Luckily, three young mares from a village called Lusitano, down near the Appleloosan Trail, had found her. They'd noticed the distinctive tree dancing in the distance and guessed it had found a target on whom to play its cruel joke. Daring Do was embarrassed at her ignorance of the species of tree, but she thanked them for their kindness. The ponies had also been generous enough to guide her to the empress, even though it put them at great personal risk. Nopony wanted to go near the empress, for she was known to bewitch random passersby and use them for her dark and twisted plots.

With his similar look, this blond pony could have been one of the noble residents of the same region, but he was still untrustworthy until proven otherwise. Daring Do sensed something was off. Especially with the smell of those peppered pears.

"Daring Do!" he bellowed into the clearing. His voice fell flat against the dense thicket of trees. "If you are anywhere in the vicinity—and I *hope* you are—it would do you well to visit the village Marapore. Before it's too late!" He turned and looked right at her hiding rock, his eyes boring into it as if it were transparent. Daring Do sucked in her breath. His voice was heavy with regret. "It may well be too late already."

"Something to help you study," the pony said, bending down to the porch. He sighed, lingering for a few more moments, his eyes searching the trees. "I wish I could explain more, but we're going to need that brilliant mind of yours if you're going to save us from him. *Please*, come save us, Daring Do." Then he galloped off into the forest with his golden mane flowing and cloak streaming out behind him.

Study hard? Save them? What in the Unicorn Mountain Range was he talking about? Daring emerged from her hiding place and trotted to her front door, her brain working overtime trying to make sense of the newfound puzzle.

"Ooof!" Daring cried out as something on the stoop caught her hoof. The pony could hardly believe her eyes when she saw it. She had just stumbled over an item she'd been trying to find for *years*. It was more precious to her than any gem-studded relics or magical healing crystal spheres. It was a book!

CHAPTER 3

Brought to Light

Daring Do smoothed the leather spine and slid *Encyclopedia Equestria: Rare Gems and Relics of the Known World, Volume E–F* onto the shelf with the twelve other volumes she already had in her collection. "Together at last," she marveled out loud. As far as she knew, her books were the only surviving copies of the ancient texts. Up until now, Daring's set had been incomplete. She had started to believe that she'd never find the elusive Volume E–F. But here it was, in perfect condition. The books seemed to take on a new life now that they were united.

Each individual volume was a different vibrant shade of the rainbow. The new addition was the color of a fiery daybreak— the last shade of orange before turning into an effervescent yellow. It bridged the color gap between the familiar volumes: the persimmon hue of Volume C–D and the bold canary shade of Volume G–H. Each spine bore two letters of the alphabet. The golden swirls and stars that adorned them danced as an excited family joined together once more.

Daring Do stepped back in awe for a moment before hungrily snatching the tome back from the shelf. She held it in her hooves reverently. This could be the key to *everything*. The answer to the great mysteries of Equestria and beyond. She must have looked in a hundred libraries all over the world for it. Why had the stranger been so eager to give it up? Daring knew enough to be wary of such gifts, but she couldn't help herself from wanting to accept this one blindly.

"Come to Daring..." she cooed, and her stomach rumbled in response. Food could wait. Daring Do took off her tan pith helmet and threw it across the room. It landed on an old, neglected typewriter on her rolltop desk in the corner. She sank down in her favorite squashy green arm-chair and slid on her red horn-rimmed reading glasses. Daring gingerly opened the hardback and smoothed over the inside cover with her hoof.

A bookplate had been pasted onto the left side. It simply said, FROM THE LIBRARY OF GR. A clue to the mysterious stallion's iden-tity, perhaps? Who was this soul who had given her this priceless book from his own collection? And, more importantly, *why*? Maybe he *was* trustworthy. Maybe she should have spoken with him, especially after that desperate cry for help for the town of Marapore. Wherever *that* was.

Daring flipped through the pages fran-tically, looking for more answers. It was difficult to do without even knowing the questions. Still, she couldn't devour the information on the pages fast enough. An hour passed. Daring had gotten side-tracked reading about something called the Elements of Harmony. Then she noticed that a page in the *F*s was dog-eared. Her hoof made its way down the old yellow parchment.

"Hmm, Fauna…Feldspar…Flankara Relics…*Great Luna!*" Daring stood up in shock. She had completely forgotten about the Flankara Relics! They were referenced in her U–V volume in the section "Vehoovius, Mount." It didn't say what they were, but it did say they were very powerful and to "see Volume E–F, 'Flankara Relics.'" She had always wondered what they were, and now she was about to discover what great power they actually bore. Daring felt as if the earth were moving beneath her hooves.

Flankara Relics: Consisting of a staff, a sword, and an arrow, these three magical items are known to provide the most powerful protection in the world (when in close proximity with one another). Alternately, the relics can be arranged in a six-pointed star formation—allowing the possessor to undo any magically inflicted injury.* Believed to be created by a great wizard. Rumored to have been found by the Stalwart Stallion of Neighples on his travels with the Royal

Navy. He gifted the relics to the Tricorner Villages of Lusitano, Marapore, and Ponypeii as a means of protection against the highly active volcano Mount Vehoovius (see Volume U–V).

*Known as the Vehoovius Hex—can only be used once. Legend says it must be witnessed by a captive audience and a "Golden Pedagogue." Owing to the single-use nature of the spell, this theory remains unproven.

See also: "Protection Spells," "Weapons."

Daring's heart began to beat faster. It always did when she was about to con- nect the dots. She raced to the bookshelf and pulled out the U–V volume, swiftly locating the section on the active volcano Mount Vehoovius.

"Aha!" Daring shouted as she reviewed the text, which told her that the mountain erupted decennially and this very year was the tenth since the volcano had last showered its surrounding areas with hot lava. "I knew it! Vehoovius is set to erupt any day!"

She felt satisfied with her detective work and worried at the same time. Whenever somepony showed up at her door with a desperate plea for help, it was a given that the mission was going to include some sort of treasure hunt. It was Daring Do's specialty, after all. But this was something more.

If his blatant call for help wasn't enough, the rumpled visitor had made things more clear with his gift—he wanted her to read about the Flankara Relics and their lifesaving powers. If the ponies of the Tricorner Villages needed Daring Do now, there was only one logical conclusion: the Flankara Relics were in grave danger. And from the sound of it, so were the residents of Lusitano, Marapore, and Ponypeii. Without their magical protection from Mount Vehoovius, what was going to stop the volcano from erupting and destroying everypony in the three towns? Daring shuddered at the

thought of it. There was only one choice.
Even though she'd just gotten home, it
was time for the great Daring Do to go on
another quest. There wasn't even time for
dinner. She just hoped she could make it
in time.

CHAPTER 4

The Get On Inn

It didn't take Daring Do long to trot, fly, and gallop her way through the winding forest toward the Appleloosan Trail. It was a perilous trek fraught with steep cliffs and rushing rivers, but surges of adrenaline brought on by the promise of a new adventure had propelled her for the last several hours.

A massive old tree with a trunk as wide as a canoe came into view in the distance. Daring rarely relied on landmarks after the wandering tree incident, but she didn't really need to—her sense of direction was impeccable. In fact, her cutie mark was a green-and-gold compass rose. But this specific tree meant she was about halfway to Mount Vehoovius and the Tricorner Villages. Her map confirmed it.

The air was beginning to chill, and the sky had turned a dusky gray, exposing a canopy of pinprick stars and a low, glowing moon. The cacophony of crickets and furry scavengers rustling through brush grew louder as the night came to life. Daring surveyed her options. She could keep heading south and arrive by sunrise, or she could take shelter for the night. After her long stint on Captain Pony's ship and her swift exit from the cottage, she was finally beginning to feel the weight of exhaustion. Whenever Daring Do could barely flap her wings, she allowed herself a short rest period of trotting. With each step she took, the weariness pulling on her hooves reminded her of the cinder blocks that were once strapped to them by Ahuizotl in an attempt to stop her from stealing the Rings of Scorchero. She had to face facts—the pony needed rest.

The surrounding trees provided adequate cover to make camp, but the cold crook of a trunk seemed less inviting than the prospect of a soft bed made up in white cotton linens. Daring Do shivered and carried on through the darkening foliage. *Just a bit farther,* she thought. *I will not surrender to something as silly as sleep.*

Soon enough, a plume of smoke could be seen puffing out from the chimney of a barn about a mile away. Daring picked up her pace to reach the front door. The Get On Inn was a little barn-and-breakfast run by a crusty old Unicorn mare named Mrs. Trotsworth. The stout patroness kept a cozy complex with ten individual barns. They were available to rent for a small nightly fee and included a hearty meal or two. Daring's mouth began to water at the thought of the scrumptious carrot-and-apple stew she'd devoured the last time she'd stopped in. The best part of the place was that Mrs. Trotsworth never asked any questions about who a pony was or where she was headed. The less said, the better, just the way Daring Do liked it. That way, nopony could get into trouble for knowing too much. An adventurer never knew who was on her tail. Daring knew that going up against Ahuizotl and Dr. Caballeron made her a target. And when a pony was a target, she couldn't keep anypony close. Working alone was the best way to avoid . . . *situations.*

Daring saw the inn through the trees. The wooden sign out front swung in the gentle breeze, creating a creaky sound like an old playground seesaw. Daring was relieved to see that the hooks below the sign bore the word VACANCY. The rocky path to the entrance crunched beneath her hooves as she walked.

Once inside, warmth enveloped the

Pegasus. She didn't even realize how chilly she'd gotten. But the stone hearth in the corner greeted her with flames crackling up against a fresh log, and she instantly felt better. Even her wing feathers had been cold.

"Hello?" Daring called out. Nopony was at the front desk. Daring rang the bell on the counter three times. *Ding, ding, ding.*

Suddenly, Mrs. Trotsworth appeared. She looked the same as the last time Daring Do had seen her—a frizzy gray mane, a red plaid country dress, and a cloth napkin with various stains on it hanging from the apron around her waist. "Back again, dearie?" she said, before erupting into a fit of coughs.

Daring nodded cordially. "Same as before." She kept her head low so that her pith helmet covered her eyes. "And send up a bowl of that stew. Please."

"Of course..." Mrs. Trotsworth replied. Her eyes began to twinkle. "And how will ye be payin' this time?" The last time Daring Do had come through here, all she'd had on her were some ancient gold coins she'd recovered from the Forgotten Palace of Tlatelolco. Daring had had no choice but to pony up a whole coin as payment. Begrudgingly, of course. She always kept smaller change with her now. As Daring procured the appropriate amount of money from her pocket, she considered that the previous gold coin should have been enough to pay for her to have the best room at the Get On Inn for a year.

"Just bits today, I'm afraid," Daring replied coolly as she tossed her payment on the counter. The coins landed with a loud clank, and Mrs. Trotsworth's expression morphed into a scowl. "Very well, then..." She gathered the coins and dropped them into the near-empty register.

The old mare busied herself puttering around behind the counter, scribbling something down on a ledger and coughing. Mrs. Trotsworth snatched a rusted key from a hook labeled #8. "Our best room," she said, like she was doing Daring a huge favor. Daring took note that all the keys were currently present on their hooks except hers and the one for room number three. She seriously doubted that all the guests were out and about this time of night, which could only mean that there were no guests. Usually the place was packed to full capacity.

"Slow week?" Daring pointed her hoof at the wall.

Mrs. Trotsworth grunted. "Same as any other lately. Business just ain't the same since all the robberies down south. No-pony wants to visit the Tricorner Villages anymore." Mrs. Trotsworth pulled out a stack of fresh towels that were looking a bit worse for wear and slid them toward Daring. "Most of my customers used to be tourists on their way to Marapore, Lusitano, or Ponypeii. I'm the closest lodging to the region. But now—nothing." She stared out the window wistfully, as if she were gazing back into better days.

"Robberies?" Daring echoed. She hadn't heard about any robberies, but the mysterious visitor had mentioned Marapore. Maybe that's what he was so worried about.

"Terrible, ain't it?" Mrs. Trotsworth sighed, back from her trance. "In fact, you're the only guest I've got tonight."

"But what about room number three?" Daring gestured to the missing key.

Mrs. Trotsworth shook her head in dismay. "A few hours back, a stallion came in wanting a room. He *insisted* on room three. Then, when I went to check on him later, he'd up and left without even so much as a good-bye! He still owed me four bits, too. Can you believe it? And I don't even want to *mention* the state of the room." She slammed a hoof on the counter and gritted her teeth. "The nerve of some ponies…"

Now she had Daring Do's attention. Maybe there was a connection between the guest and her own visitor. Daring leaned in closer and brought her voice to a low rasp. "Was he wearing a green cloak, perchance? Messy golden mane?"

"Well, I think he had on a—" Mrs. Trotsworth stopped herself and looked at Daring Do sideways. "What's it to ya?" Daring Do needed to tone it down with the nosy questions, otherwise she might reveal something confidential. The last thing she needed right now was to have to explain her mission to somepony. She fumbled for another coin and tossed it to the old mare. That ought to loosen her lips a bit.

"Yeah, I remember now…" said Mrs. Trotsworth, inspecting the prize with a cheeky smirk. "He *did* have on a green cloak. What else ya want to know?"

Daring smiled back. "Let's talk about it on our way to room number three."

CHAPTER 5
Room Number Three

It was no wonder the innkeeper was perturbed. The room was an absolute mess. The bedsheets had been torn off the mattress and thrown across the floor. The plush pillows had been ripped apart, and the white feathers had exploded everywhere, causing the entire place to look like it had gotten almost an inch of downy snow. The flickering bedside lamp was overturned, and there was a trail of muddy hoofprints tracked all over the wooden panels of the barn floor. The work of a ruffian. One of Caballeron's men? It was his henchponies who had trashed her cottage while searching for the last Ring of Scorchero.

"Looks like somepony *wasn't* raised in a barn," Daring Do said aloud, peeking under the tousled blankets. The innkeeper sniffed and left Daring Do alone to dig around.

After Daring Do had searched the whole room high and low, she was incredibly disappointed. All she'd found was an old, half-used jar of Goops for Stuff

Hide Ointment and a crumpled piece of parchment with some circles scribbled on it. They meant nothing to her, but she stashed them in her bag anyway. It seemed that cloaked pony had simply forgotten them on the table in the madness of it all. It was too bad that he'd left no other clues in his wake.

The next morning, Daring Do awoke before dawn to find that her body was stiffer than the board on a pirate ship's plank. It was as if each wing and limb had been bound with rope and tied to a sand-bag. Though it was the first time in weeks she'd had a full night of sleep, it wasn't restful. She tossed and turned throughout the night, her mind hijacked by a disturbing dream that she'd been surrounded by hundreds of little animals crying out for her. She tried to shake the odd feeling it gave her, but she could still imagine their fuzzy faces and watery eyes. "Save us, Daring Do!" they pleaded. The plea mixed with that of the stranger's and swirled above her head like a gray rain cloud.

A sliver of morning light began to peek through the burlap curtains. Daring was about to go draw a hot bath to loosen up before she took off again, when a jar on the nightstand caught her attention. It was the hide ointment that had been left behind in room three. *No time for a bath,* she thought. *This will do perfectly to ease my aching muscles until I can relax.* She scooped out a generous portion of the oily green goop and slathered it on her green-and-gold compass rose cutie mark. It smelled a bit sour. Daring looked at the jar again. Nothing on the bottle indicated it had gone bad. She shrugged.

She rubbed the stuff in and made sure that it soaked into her flank and hind legs. A moment later, a tingling sensation took over, and she was able to stretch and walk once more. Daring Do was back in action and ready to save some ponies by finding those Flankara Relics. That is, if a certain raider hadn't gotten there first.

CHAPTER 6
Enter the Jungle

Warm winds rushed through Daring Do's gray-and-black mane as she zipped across the late-morning sky, legs outstretched, reaching toward her destiny. It had been a rough flight from the inn, but she'd flown straight there with no stops. She couldn't waste any more precious time with silly matters like rest. There would be no helping ponies if they were already eternally frozen in volcanic ash and cinders.

Daring Do applauded herself for her impeccable sense of direction and fast flying as Mount Vehoovius came into view. As she soared through the atmosphere toward the behemoth, Daring Do felt like the wind had been knocked from her lungs. Vehoovius was the largest volcano she'd ever seen! It reached far up into the clouds, kissing the blue sky. The blackened, sloping sides had formed deep grooves from the repeated expulsion of hot, molten lava throughout the millions of years of its existence. Patches of green foliage creeping up the wide base of the formation were a dead giveaway that it had been several years since its last eruption. That meant she'd made it here in time! She still had a fighting chance at finding the relics and returning them to their rightful places before disaster struck.

The volcano was beautiful, yet daunting. Daring Do wondered how the ponies of this region had managed to build their towns here with such an imminent threat dictating their entire lives. There were no other towns or cities for hundreds of miles in each direction. Back at the inn, Mrs. Trotsworth had explained that the citizens of the Tricorner Villages were so remote from everypony else that they'd created their own fully functioning society. The three towns were each in charge of a major resource, and they shared their bounty with one another. The residents of Ponypeii were the farmers, the ponies of Lusitano lived near the river and thus provided fresh water, and those who lived in Marapore were the masters of the loom, providing the distinctive cloaks of the region.

The ponies of Marapore's talents were rumored to be entirely in their creation of the special garments, which tourists to the region coveted. Some ponies said the cloaks were magical and gave the wearer unique powers. Daring wasn't sure what she believed. But a well-traveled voyager such as herself had seen many far-fetched things—temples crumbling to the ground in three seconds flat, natives shooting a hundred poison-tipped arrows at her as she weaved through the forest, and massive boulders chasing her down narrow underground passageways. Whatever the truth was about the mysterious villagers, all signs pointed to Marapore as the place to start looking for it.

Daring tilted her body, soaring through the low-hanging clouds and perusing the gradient of rich greens below for the ideal place to touch down. She wanted to land just outside Marapore so that she could get hold of her bearings before entering the town. If anypony noticed her prematurely, she might have to explain herself. Sometimes the quickest way to ruin a mission was to make it known to the public. Questions demanded answers.

The scene seemed to be accurate to

the map she'd obtained in her *Atlas of Equestria*. The base of Mount Vehoovius was surrounded by thick tropical foliage, a blanket of deep greens, fiery reds, and rich purples. A worn path connecting the three towns forged a visible triangle from the sky, with the staggering mountain rising up from the center.

Along the side of one of the villages was a sparkling turquoise river, which meant it must be Lusitano. Daring flapped her wings harder, circling around to make her way to the next village. A colored patchwork of crop fields implied that the land belonged to the farmers of Ponypeii. Daring flew on toward the final point of the triangle. As she came in closer, she could make out a tiny grid of clay cottages with green-and-beige thatched roofs. *Definitely Marapore*, Daring thought, recalling an illustration on the wall at the Get On Inn.

A surge of excitement rushed through Daring's body. It wouldn't be long until she would find this shadowy, cloaked pony and have him lead her to the priceless Flankara Relics. This quest was extremely dangerous, but she was up for the challenge. Daring dived down into the hot jungle, just outside the town. She spread her golden wings, landing gracefully next to a group of wide-trunked palm trees. Their long green fronds swayed gently in the light breeze, which offered the only relief from the tropical atmosphere. It was a stunning scene, if stifling heat and impending fiery doom was your sort of thing.

The scent from the native hibiscus flowers was so strong she could almost see it. Daring breathed in the sweet, intoxicating air and then remembered what she'd read about the vegetation in this part of the world. Thousands of breeds of exotic flowers were common here, especially somnambular blooms. She gathered one of the massive fuchsia flowers in her hoof and checked the stem to make sure it wasn't orange. If so, she'd be asleep in moments, even though she would look like she was awake. It would be pointless to sleepwalk through her whole adventure, not to mention dangerous. Luckily, the stem was just a harmless, pleasing shade of purple. Daring Do took another hearty whiff and let the freshness fill her lungs.

A bead of sweat dripped down her face, and a lock of black mane clung to the nape of her neck. Daring removed her pith helmet and stashed it in a patch of ferns and bushes with lavender leaves as big as her body. It was far too humid for headwear at the moment, plus it drew too much attention. For now, blending in was of utmost importance.

There were several identifiable land-marks, including a glistening aqua pond and three palms of exactly the same height in a row. She checked the roots to make sure that they weren't wanderers, and whipped out a piece of chalk from her shirt pocket. A scribbled X on the middle tree would suffice.

The sound of a white-feathered ghost macaw echoed through the trees.

"Caaaaaacaaaaaaaw!" The great bird spread its frosted wings and whooshed past Daring Do. Was that a warning or a welcome? No matter; it didn't deter her. She was here to do a job, and nothing would stand in her way. Not even the deadliest tropical bird known to ponykind.

"What do we have here?" Daring mumbled to herself, inspecting a set of large hoofprints in the dried mud. There were two straight lines on either side—the impressions from many carts traveling through. It was part of the trade route she'd seen from above.

The pony dug into her brown satchel and pulled out a light silver hooded robe. It was the closest thing to a Marapore cloak she'd been able to find in her closet back home. With any luck, the disguise would allow her to do some investigating without getting noticed as a foreigner. Urban camouflage was an art—Daring found it even more of a challenge than hiding away in a bunch of plants. This time, she was also a Pegasus in mainly Earth pony territory. She would have to keep her wings in tight for the time being.

A low hiss came from the bushes. Daring Do froze in her tracks. Jungles were vast, treacherous places with plenty of nooks and crannies for deadly creatures to hide in. Daring Do had more than once found herself being trailed by a predator or two. The culprit was revealed when a gigantic green snake slithered underhoof. The sun shone through the treetops in shafts, glinting onto the creature's shiny scales. However, the snake seemed entirely uninterested in the pony adventurer. He disappeared into the foliage with another hiss as punctuation.

"Phew!" Daring continued on, hooves padding quietly against the dried mud and fallen palm frond–covered ground. She was starting to think she'd miscalculated her proximity to the town when muffled sounds of many ponies gathered in one place rumbled through the trees. *Perfect*, she thought. *A crowd is the best place to go unnoticed.*

"Filly-ho!" she said to herself as she forged ahead, picking up the pace into a full gallop. Dust and fern leaves rustled under her hooves as she ran, speeding ahead toward what appeared to be a sunny clearing. She only realized her mistake when it was almost too late. She was headed straight over a cliff!

The village was directly below, about forty feet down. Her hooves came to a screeching halt beneath her, trying to gain purchase on the leafy ground. "Whoaaa!" she called out as she extended her wings as a reflex. She flapped them gently and backed herself away from the edge. Her cloak had fallen back from her face and away from her wings. Daring was completely exposed. Everypony stopped the rhythmic chanting she had overheard and looked up at her. Their eyes, which were still wet with tears, now grew wide with awe.

"The Golden Prophesied Pegasus!" a tall blue pony in a magenta cloak cried out. "We're saved!"

So much for an inconspicuous entrance.

CHAPTER 7
The Golden Prophesied Pegasus

The villagers encircled her, buzzing with excited chatter. "I think you have the wrong pony," Daring Do pleaded as an old granny took her by the hoof. The mare mumbled something incoherent as she led the perplexed Daring into the town. "I'm not the Pegasus you seek. I am a mere..." Daring racked her brain. For some reason, A. B. Ravenhoof popped into her mind. "I'm just…a teacher!" This statement seemed to excite them more. They stomped their hooves on the dirt in applause.

"Welcome to Marapore. I am the one they call Kaaxtik," said the tall blue pony as he stepped forward. "We've been expecting you"—he bowed to her in respect—"oh wise one."

Kaaxtik pushed back his hood to reveal an intricately braided white mane. At the end of each braid, a tiny sculpted crystal was woven in. His silken cloak looked as smooth as butter and was the color of a beautiful sunset. The fabric shimmered in a way that Daring Do had never beheld in all her travels. Even the green leaf-patterned trim looked as if it were a living, breathing plant, reaching its vines out and growing with time. Maybe the cloak did have magical properties. Kaaxtik was clearly an important pony to be wearing such finery.

"Bad things have happened here." He shook his head in despair and looked down at the ground. Kaaxtik put his arm around Daring and whispered in her ear, "Unspeakable things."

Daring perked up. She leaned toward Kaaxtik and whispered, "Does this have anything to do with the Flankara Relics?"

"It has everything to do with them." Kaaxtik nodded sagely. The crystals in his braids shimmered in the sunlight.

"Can you lead me to one of them?"

Daring Do asked, her voice breathy with anticipation. She was on the brink of something. "The sword, the staff...or the arrow?" If only she could just *see* one of the legendary items, she might have some idea about how to retrieve the others. Then the villages might be safe from Vehoovius's eruption.

"I wish I could show all of them to you..." Kaaxtik said, his voice dripping with dramatic sorrow. "But the protector of the relics—our schoolteacher, Golden Rule—has been ponynapped! Along with the Staff of Ponypeii and the Sword of Lusitano, I'm afraid. The Arrow of Marapore still rests here."

"Where?" Daring demanded, looking around in a panic.

Kaaxtik ignored her and replied, "It is an immeasurable blessing that you should find yourself on our doorstep. One that cannot mean nothing." He bowed to her again, his forelegs touching the ground. The villagers followed suit, bowing down.

"What are you getting at?" Daring Do replied. These locals sure did know how to beat around the bush.

"You must stay here and take over his role as protector of the relics…and as the schoolteacher of Marapore." Kaaxtik shrugged with a smile. "Then maybe you will get the answers you seek."

"Me? Teach?" Daring Do didn't want to disappoint the ponies of Marapore, and she was going to need these ponies to cooperate with her. How else would she get close to the Flankara Relics? She hadn't technically been lying when she said she'd been a teacher at one time. It was just a short stint with A. B. Ravenhoof at the university, but it still counted. She'd often thought of going back, but the call of adventure was far too great for her to settle down in some dusty classroom trying to explain important things to young ponies who didn't seem to care much.

"Kaaxtik, you drive a hard bargain." She cocked her head to the side and rolled her eyes. "But I'll do it." Kaaxtik nodded his head with a grin.

Daring Do knew he must have seen many like her before—along with helping ponies, treasure hunters were often in it for the thrill of the chase. It was mostly about the quest, the glory of finding something extraordinary. They would do almost anything to achieve their goals, even if the prize wasn't something they planned to keep. He could tell she was hungry to find the Flankara Relics.

What she didn't know was that he thought that whether she was the true prophesied Pegasus was irrelevant. She was all he had and, as the village leader, Kaaxtik had to look out for morale.

"Ponies of Marapore," Kaaxtik bellowed, facing the eager crowd. With all their cloaks, their bodies appeared as a sea of shimmering fabrics. He raised his hooves high in the air. "We have prayed to the great guardians, and they have answered us. Let us be grateful that we have nothing left to fear. For it is prophe-sied that a foreign pony of vast knowledge will arrive in our hour of need." Kaax-tik held up Daring's hoof in triumph. "It has happened! This golden-winged angel shall protect us!" The ponies cheered and hugged one another. A small lemon-colored filly wearing a patchy olive cloak trotted up and laid a single hibiscus flower at Daring's hooves. She looked up at the adventurer, doe-eyed. "For you, Maid... um...what's your name?"

"Um..." Daring Do raised an eyebrow. Maybe she could still salvage some ano-nymity. "The name's Ravenhoof. Mare-ion Ravenhoof."

CHAPTER 8
The Wisdom of Colts and Scholars

The surface of the blackboard emitted a high-pitched screech as Daring Do dragged a piece of yellow chalk across it. She took no notice of the wincing she'd caused among her pupils and continued scribbling furiously. The tiny schoolroom behind her was packed with young fillies and colts trying to follow the adventurer's lesson, but failing miserably. It was probably because three minutes into her lecture on the mechanics of active volcanoes, she forgot she was supposed to be teaching and careened off into a faraway, dangerous place—the corners of her mind. Because once Daring Do started theorizing the whereabouts of a certain prize and how to obtain it, she was not responsible for where her thoughts took her. Usually this didn't take place in front of an audience, though.

Screeeeeeech. The students winced again as Daring's hoof scratched the chalk on the board. She mumbled quietly like a mathematician on the brink of a brilliant new theorem. The picture she'd drawn of the Sword of Lusitano had been circled twelve times, and arrows pointed across the board to different notes and drawings. She put her hoof to her chin. "But if the relics are connected, then why would they still work once apart? If what this book says is true, the power is only accessible through the joining of all three in this formation and the witnessing of this act by a 'Golden Pedagogue.'"

She pointed to a diagram she'd drawn of the relics in a six-pointed star shape. "But maybe they have a different power from reversing an injury? We already know that they protect the three villages from Mount Vehoovius...who's to neigh that there aren't even *more* purposes—"

"Miss Ravenhoof?" a diminutive voice

squeaked from the back of the room. Daring Do paced back and forth. She leaned down to a table filled with various reference books on Tricorner history. The school had provided a wealth of information on the Flankara Relics, but some of the books were hoofwritten and extremely old. In all likelihood, they were the only existing copies. But certain pages were missing, which made it very difficult to piece together the mystery. She turned the page on a bound set of scrolls titled *Protective Powers of the Empire.* Her eyes scanned the old tome, trying to make the connections. A set of words on the page suddenly jumped out at her: *Stalwart Stallion of Neighples.* It was as if she'd been hanging off the side of a tall cliff and finally found a hoofhold to pull herself up with. Where had she just read that?

"Miss Ravenhoof!" the colt said again, louder. His desk scooted around as he fidgeted, hoof raised in a desperate attempt to attract attention. The thought flew away faster than a heron that'd spotted a thrashing salmon. Daring slumped down, annoyed. So close. "What is it? Can't you see I'm a bit busy?"

"It's just that…I think I can help." The colt lowered his hoof, a knowing grin on his tiny face. His coat was light brown, and upon his head was a messy chocolate-colored mane. He hadn't grown into his tail yet—it sprouted out like a little plant. Freckles were sprayed across the bridge of his muzzle. Like the other students, he wore his blue school vest, but he also had added his own flair—a red baseball cap with a star on the front. Who knew where he'd obtained such a piece of clothing. It was definitely not from anywhere near here.

"Kid, no offense," Daring Do replied, "but I think I've got this." The pony turned back to the chalkboard and started scribbling some words that made no sense, even to her.

"You don't even want to hear what I have to say, Miss Ravenhoof?" the colt asked, twirling his quill. The hopeful expression on his face and the fact that Daring Do had already lost all her leads on any sort of coherent theory made her reconsider. She plopped down at the teacher's desk, defeated.

"Fine," she offered. She leaned back, propped her hind legs on her desk, and took a bite of a fresh-cut pineapple one of the students had brought as an offering for the "Prophesied Pegasus." The deliciously sweet tanginess of the fruit delighted her taste buds. Juice started to run down her chin, but she didn't even care. "Let's hear it, then."

The rest of the class had stopped trying to pay attention by now, anyway. The sad excuse for a ceiling fan, made of flimsy palm tree fronds, was losing the war against the humidity. Half the students were asleep, and the other half were busy passing notes to one another. A paper Pegasus flew through the stuffy air, out the open window, and straight into a patch of turquoise xihuitl grass. A tan filly with braided pigtails up front was drawing a picture of a bunny. At the top, she'd written: MY PET, FLUFFY BUN.

"You had it right. It's the Stalwart Stallion of Neighples," the colt said matter-of-factly. He pointed to a corner of the blackboard where Daring Do had drawn a picture of the town statue, the keeper of the Arrow of Marapore. "Well, his real name is Mojo, but he's the thief. See, he used to be a good guy. He's the one who brought the Flankara Relics to Tricorner, but he's really mad now, so he wants them back. Except nopony in town believes me that it's him. They all just like him so much."

Daring scoffed. Why would the guy who'd gifted the town the relics take them back? She cocked an eyebrow. "I'm not sure I follow you, pipsqueak...."

"My name's Tater Tot! I'll show you," the colt replied. He got up from his desk and trotted to the front. He began to riffle through the books, clearly familiar with the old texts. "GR used to let me look at these after class," he explained, flipping a yellowed page.

"GR?" Daring pictured the hoofwriting on the inside cover of the encyclopedia volume back home. FROM THE LIBRARY OF GR, it said. "Who is this GR exactly?"

"Our real teacher, Golden Rule." Tater Tot shrugged. The little pony kept flipping through the pages. "He's like some sort of supersmart relic scholar. Before he was taken, he taught me all this stuff."

Tater Tot gestured to the blackboard and the stack of books.

Golden Rule. *Golden Pedagogue. Pedagogue* was just a fancy word for *teacher*. It made sense now—Golden Rule was to be the witness to the Vehoovius Hex!

Daring Do tried to recall the face of the golden-maned pony who'd paid her a visit. It had to have been Golden Rule! After all, he had a golden mane and tail and his cutie mark was a ruler. This extensive library at the school did seem like a place the last volume of the encyclopedia could have been hiding. And she would never have known to come down here until she'd made the connection from the missing book! The clever stallion had left it as a clue.

After all, his gift had included the information on the Flankara Relics. He had been trying to lure her to Marapore to help save his kinsponies. But that didn't explain why he'd trashed room number three at the Get On Inn, leaving her nothing but some ointment and a used piece of paper. Or why Mojo would have let Golden Rule, his only ticket to completing the Vehoovius Hex, out of his sight.

"Aha! Here it is!" Tater Tot cried out in delight, smoothing down the page of what appeared to be the oldest book in the stack. Pieces of certain pages had been torn out, and an entire chapter in the beginning was missing. "'Half past stars marks the hour, masked by darkness of the night. Foal once noble now turned

sour, will try to bring the fire and light.' "
He looked up at her, proud of himself, as if
the words made perfect sense and weren't
penned in some cryptic code.

"Makes sense." Daring scratched her
chin again as she reread the rhyme. One
thing was for sure: The words *fire* and *light*
were not ideal ones when you lived at the
base of an active volcano. Mojo was definitely going to try to use the power of
Vehoovius to complete the hex. Which
meant that so far, all her theories had been
spot-on. It was encouraging to hear them
confirmed by the colt. Daring narrowed her
eyes at Tater Tot. "What else do you know?"

"Mojo needs a 'captive audience.' The
pets of Marapore are about to disappear,"
Tater Tot replied, eyes growing wide. He

paused and looked around. None of the other students were paying any mind. "Oh, and I know that your name isn't Miss Ravenhoof." He lowered his voice to a whisper. "It's Daring Do, huh?"

"Heeeeeelp!" a shrill voice rang out. It was coming from outside in the square. The pitter-patter of hundreds of hoof-beats rumbled as the villagers ran from their homes and workplaces to see what new travesty had befallen their beloved Marapore.

"Heeeeeelp!" called the lean young mare again. Tears were streaming down her white face. She let out a sob. An older mare, presumably her mother, rubbed the pony's back and cooed, "What is it, Yollotl?"

"He…he…he's goooone! My little Bruno is gone! He was just a puppy…." She heaved again, sobbing. Kaaxtik passed her a sky-blue hoofkerchief. Yollotl blew her muzzle, and the unpleasant sound that followed was like that of a large goose.

"I haven't seen any of my kitties all day…." said a colt, about to erupt into a puddle of despair.

"Where is Fluffy BUUUUN?!" the tan pigtailed filly cried, running off with her unfinished drawing of the dear bunny still in her hoof.

A stallion in a red cloak stepped up to join them and added, "My goose is nowhere to be seen!"

Yollotl blew her muzzle again.

"Denise, is that you?!" The stallion looked around in confusion.

"Sorry, just me," Yollotl said sadly.

Kaaxtik hung his head for a moment and looked up to the villagers. "It is just as we feared, perhaps much worse. Everypony go to your homes and take the necessary precautions." The ponies stared back with blank faces. "Quickly!" Panic set in, and everypony scrambled, running for their dwellings.

Daring Do and Tater Tot exchanged a look as the commotion swirled around them. If the rest of the predictions were going to come true, tonight was the night. They both knew it.

"Come on, kid. We've got work to do." Daring passed him the crumpled piece of paper with the circles on it. The one she'd found at the barn-and-breakfast. "Any notions as to what this means?"

Tater Tot snatched the paper, and his eyes lit up with delight. "Well, I don't know what it says, but I know where it came from."

A few minutes later, they'd located the book. The ripped corner fit perfectly onto page thirty-three of *Prophesies of the Southern Region: Tricorner Villages*, just like a puzzle piece. Without the extra bit, the page was totally undecipherable, but together, it made complete sense.

Daring gasped as the realization hit her.

The illustration on the page showed a pony knocking his hoof on the mouth of a cave. In the next panel, a door appeared. The circles were some kind of password written in Horse code! The way it worked was simple. A pony had to do a series of hoof knocks varying in length, one after another, to be admitted through the hidden door. Now all she needed was to find that door.

A smile crept over Daring's face. The only thing between her and her goal now was a single pony named Mojo. And she would bet every bit she owned that she knew where he would turn up tonight. All Daring had to do was wait for him to get there.

CHAPTER 9
Half Past Stars Marks the Hour

The Marapore village square was cloaked in night, the buildings a canvas of alternating shadows and shades of blue. The air was beginning to cool. And a yellow Pegasus with a gray-and-black mane sat waiting patiently. She had never been more ready.

Daring stared down at her hooves and practiced the pattern of Horse code from the paper. Once she'd perfected that, she looked up at the stars and passed the time by listening to the symphonic scratch of crickets. If it weren't for the fact that the cottage windows had all been hastily boarded up with firewood, the soft snores of the ponies in their beds would have added some percussion to the score. Daring shifted her body weight to make more room for her wings. She had chosen to wait in the school doorway because it had the perfect view of the village square.

Daring recited the rhyme in her head again. *Half past stars marks the hour, masked by darkness of the night.* "Half past stars," Daring mumbled to herself, considering that maybe she'd missed something in the message. "Easy. Has to be a half hour past sundown." The "darkness of the night" thing was obvious, too. *Foal once noble now turned sour.* More open to interpretation than the others, but if that kid knew what he was talking about, the phrase did imply the possibility of a local hero gone bad being the culprit. And the only pony who fit that bill was Mojo, also known as the Stalwart Stallion of Neighples. The reason *why* he'd turned sour was an entirely separate issue.

Daring Do still couldn't believe how much Tater Tot had known about the prophecy, the Flankara Relics, and their infinite powers. His insatiable thirst for knowledge reminded Daring a little bit of herself at that age: curious to the point of recklessness. Anything for an adventure. It was endearing, really. But following a hero turned evil thief in the middle of the night was not something that little tyke should be doing.

Tater Tot had begged to come along, but she told him to scram. Too many younger ponies thought they had the chops to do what Daring did on a daily basis, and too many got caught in the cross fire. They always needed rescuing in the end. It was exactly why she preferred to work alone.

Daring exhaled deeply. Of all the parts of her job, stakeouts were the worst. If no-pony showed up soon, she was just going to have to go out and take some action herself. Finding the cave door and kicking some stallion flank both seemed like appealing options. She crept out from her hiding place, keeping her knees bent low to the ground in her signature crawl. The village square wasn't wide, so with only a few paces she was in front of the statue.

In the moonlight, the stone sculpture took on a new life. During the day, it had looked proud and valiant. Now it seemed ominous. The eyes of the stallion were wet with night dew, creepily glistening like real eyes. One could have mistaken them for actual salty tears. Daring reached her hoof up to touch the moisture, just to be sure. It was never a good sign when things made of stone cried. Daring knew *that* one from experience.

The sight of rain running down the eyes of the statue on the Hidden Tomb of the Cipactli Queen was forever burned into her memory. She imagined it was tears dripping into the crevices and the sounds of screams that had given away the band of Caballeron's henchponies watching from the shadows.

"What happened to you, Mojo?" Daring circled the statue. The front right hoof was frozen in a permanent raised position. Secured firmly inside the statue's grip was the mighty Arrow of Marapore. The arrow itself was made of complex, interlocking pieces of gold and silver. The relic sparkled, almost as if it were glowing from within. Daring could feel the excitement rising in her. The powers of this object were vast. A tiny part of her wanted to snatch the object for herself and fly off into the night. It was like a beautiful siren calling out to her, trying to lead her astray.

If it looked this incredible now, what had the brilliant artifact looked like before its brothers had been taken from Lusitano and Ponypeii? The three were tied to one another by some powerful, ancient spell. And the villagers had attested to the fact that the arrow had dimmed, much like their spirits, ever since Mojo had paid the other towns a visit. But why, out of the three, had the arrow remained untouched until now? There were so many questions to be answered and only one way to find out. Daring was going to watch over this monument until something happened.

The thud of hooves on the dirt path broke the silence. Daring darted back to her hiding spot, her heart beating wildly in her chest. She covered her mouth with her cloak to muffle her breathing. Everything was unfolding just as she'd hoped.

A huge stallion entered the square, his form dark and menacing against the star-filled sky. The shaggy base of each of his hooves was as big as all four of Daring Do's put together, and with each stomp, the ground rattled beneath him. As he drew closer, details of his countenance came into sharp focus. Daring craned to see his cutie mark, but he kept moving back and forth—presumably to check for spies such as herself—just before she could get a glimpse of it. His hide was a shiny silver hue, and the hair of his tail was deepest black, except at the root. There, it was a putrid, glowing green.

"The Stalwart Stallion of Neighples! What a joke I must be now," the stallion bellowed as he arrived at the foot of the statue. "I never deserved a monument. It's so much more fitting that I am the great and powerful Mojo now—a pony who sees what he wants and takes it for himself!" The greedy monster looked up and unleashed a hearty cackle. "May this statue be a good warning to those who ever think of crossing me again!"

Another of Tater Tot's predictions had come true. The thief was none other than the venerated hero of the Tri-corner Villages—the Stalwart Stallion of

Neighples! The one who'd brought the Flankara Relics to the region in the first place, to protect its ponies from the lava of Mount Vehoovius. But what had made him turn evil? All this pony used to care about was protecting the villages, and now he was the one tearing them apart. It just didn't add up. Daring immediately thought of the inscription in the book, which predicted a "foal once noble now turned sour." *Sour* was an understatement. But something must have happened to scar his soul so deeply.

Then the Unicorn turned so his flank was visible, and Daring cringed, finally understanding what he was after.

His cutie mark had been mutilated. A slash down the middle had left it brutally deformed. It was difficult to tell what the symbol had been before, but it looked like it was green. The flesh in the middle was a raw, shiny red. Daring was appalled. Who would do such a thing, and how? A cutie mark was a pony's essence, a physical embodiment of their spirit. It must have been some very dark magic.

She felt an ounce of compassion for the stallion, but promptly brushed it aside. It didn't matter what he had been through; there was no way he was taking everypony down with him. The Tricorner Villages needed the Flankara Relics more than he did.

A low, booming noise resounded. It seemed like it was coming from the direction of the jungle. At first, Daring believed it to be an army barreling toward them, but the smell of sulfur and the smoke rising in the distance told her otherwise. Mount Vehoovius was going to erupt tonight!

Mojo pulled back the hood of his cloak to reveal a wild mane and yellow eyes that seemed to burn with a hunger for vengeance. He stared up at his prize with longing, but hesitated. He was savoring the moment. "I'm taking back what is rightfully mine, and nopony can stop me."

The Flankara Relics, the villages of Marapore, Lusitano, and Ponypeii, and all the ponies living there were about to become ancient history. Or they would have if Daring Do hadn't been lurking in the shadows. . . .

CHAPTER 10

The Magnificent Arrow of Marapore

Daring Do stalked behind the stallion. Thanks to the newly camouflaged cloak she'd bought that afternoon in the market, she was even more stealthy than usual. But there wasn't much time to come up with a strategy. If she jumped out and made herself known, she could certainly distract Mojo from stealing the arrow, but the consequences could be worse. He had powerful magic, magic that he would not hesitate to use on her. And she needed to stay alive if she was going to save all these other ponies. She drew closer, playing with fire, but the deranged Unicorn was far too focused on his task to see anything other than the precious object of his affection. Daring decided to follow him back to his lair.

Mojo's horn sparkled with magical light as he closed his eyes, mumbling an incantation. The shimmering arrow jostled in its spot, but it took several tries to free it. Sparks flew from the tip of his horn as if it were misfiring. He growled in anger, trying again to concentrate and aim it toward the statue. Had something happened to his magic? Daring had read studies of the link between Unicorns and their cutie marks and wondered if Mojo might be a prime example of the phenomenon.

Even so, the irony was not lost on Daring Do that Mojo was probably the one who'd placed the arrow there in the first place and, in doing so, made it extremely difficult for anypony to take it.

The arrow floated up in the air. It twirled, surrounded by black smoke. Mojo smiled. "Daring Doooo!" he singsonged. "I can see youuuu!"

"That's convenient, Mojo." Daring Do took a defensive stance, legs wide on the ground and head down. She was ready to attack. "Then you can watch as I take that arrow back off your hooves!" Daring sprang forward in a great leap, letting her wings assist her. She landed on the back of the statue and took off once more, this time aiming for the Unicorn's back. If she was behind him, he couldn't even attempt to aim his magic at her.

But Mojo darted out of the way just in time, galloping behind the schoolhouse. Daring did not falter. She flew over the one-story structure and hovered above him. "Just because something was once yours does not make it so forever, Mojo!" Daring called down.

"It doesn't?" Mojo laughed. "Well, thanks for that inspiring lesson, Professor. I think I have learned quite a lot here today." The stallion lunged forward and grabbed on to something in the shadows. The darkened mass wriggled and squirmed, but Daring knew what it was from the unmistakable red baseball cap.

"Tater Tot!" Daring cried out, feeling more than she thought she would. *Reckless kid*. Tater Tot had been watching from across the street. Of course he hadn't heeded the adventurer's warnings to stay out of the way.

"Do I have something of yours that you want back?" Mojo dragged the poor colt into the light. The little guy kicked and struggled against the great Unicorn's strength, but it was just too much for him. Mojo held a hoof over the kid's mouth.

"Well, why don't you come and get it?!"
Mount Vehoovius thundered again, and
a billow of black smoke engulfed the Unicorn and the colt. When it cleared, they
were gone.

CHAPTER 11
The Hollowed Hideout

Mojo galloped with gaining speed through the thick brush of the jungle. Tater Tot was on his back, and the Arrow of Marapore was tucked safely in a brown leather quiver looped across his broad chest. They were drawing closer to the edge of the mountain with every step.

"I'm n-n-not a-a-afraid of you!" squeaked Tater Tot, though he was shaking like a Maraporean leaf bug. "In fact, I'm h-h-having fun!"

"Excellent!" yelled Mojo, barely audible over the sound of his own hooves beating on the ground. "I always do enjoy a willing victim!"

A few miles away, Daring soared low through the canopy of palms. She was afraid that if she went any higher into the atmosphere, she'd miss her target due to the dense plant cover below. It was possible that Mojo had transported Tater Tot directly into the volcanic lair with his magic black smoke, but Daring's instincts told her that he wouldn't have made it that easy. The Unicorn wanted to be caught— he was playing with her.

"If a game is what you want, Mojo, then you'll get it!" Daring bellowed into the shadowy jungle, legs outstretched, the wind rushing past her face and through her gray-and-black mane as she wove between the trees. "And that's not all!" She swooped down a familiar row of palms, snatched her pith helmet, and slapped it on her head without slowing down.

Up ahead, Daring spotted a dense patch of hanging vines right on her course. She didn't miss a beat, reaching out to use them to swing through the jungle in a calculated rhythm. *Swing, then catch. Wings, then hoof. Swing, then catch. Wings, then hoof.* On the last one, she cast her body through the air in an effortless arc, finishing the acrobatic performance by landing on all four hooves. When she stood up, she was directly in front of a cave at the foot of the mountain. The stench of sulfur and volcanic ash wafted through the air. "I win this round, Mojo."

She entered the cave and saw a doorway on the far wall. It appeared exactly as it had in the drawing—as part of the wall, following every curve and imperfection of the natural stone formations. There was a thin layer of moss, but the outline of the entrance was almost invisible to the naked eye. Daring knew where to look. She had the torn piece of the book page in her cloak pocket, but she didn't need it. She lifted her right hoof and repeated the Horse code sequence from memory. *Tap-tap-tap. Taaaap. Tap-tap. Taaaaaap-Tap-Tap.* The entire cave began to shake, and tiny shards of volcanic rock rained down from the ceiling. Daring covered her head and looked to the door. She tried to push on it, but nothing was working. It was stuck after opening only a few inches.

There was only one thing to do. Daring ran to the other side of the cave. She tried to put as much space as possible between herself and the door, but unfortunately it was a tight space. She lunged back on her hind legs and took off as fast as her hooves would go across the length of the hollow. *Thud!* Her body slammed against the door. It rumbled slightly and then stopped. Daring sighed. That was supposed to have done the trick.

"Oooo! Ooo! Ahhhh! Eeee-yeee!" Daring Do whipped around and found herself face-to-face with none other than a blood-eyed howler monkey! She'd never seen one in real life before.

"Really?" Daring Do replied in annoyance. Though she was fascinated by its shimmering long fur and curled tail, *now* was not the time for an animal observation mission.

The monkey bared its sharp teeth and whooped again. "Eeee-yeeeee! Ahh! Ahh!" Twenty more monkeys, all swinging and screeching in fury, skulked out of the shadows. Apparently the Pegasus had accidentally disturbed someone else's lair.

"All right, fur balls. Come at me!" Daring Do took a step forward, prepared to fight off each one if she had to. But rather than fighting off the small army of angry monkeys, she suddenly found herself falling, darkness enveloping her.

A few seconds later, she landed hard on some slippery red mud. Daring careened down a narrow underground tunnel. She was heading deep into the belly of the volcano. Daring pulled her limbs in close, knowing that she could go even faster if she was streamlined. Time was running out—if she didn't save Tater Tot soon, he'd be nothing more than a crispy colt. She just hoped this tunnel didn't spit her into a pool of lava, or she'd have the same problem.

WHAM!

Daring Do hit the ground, angling her body to avoid landing on her bad wing. The shallow, sulfuric air or perhaps the fall itself made her lungs begin to seize up. A fit of uncontrollable coughs expelled themselves from the pony and echoed across the cavernous interior of ruddy volcanic mud and dripping water. Daring's dirtied cloak was tangled around her waist. If only she could reach her flagon of water from her utility pocket, she'd stop coughing. There was no way of knowing if Mojo was waiting just around the corner, ready to pounce on her while she was down. It was not a good idea to make so much noise.

But it was already too late. She'd been heard.

A legion of fluffy and feathered creatures came at her from all directions and bore down on the fallen hero. Puppies, kittens, and birdies of every breed were barking, hissing, and squawking. Each one seemed filled with nothing but an urgent desire to destroy her. Their eyes had glazed over bright yellow, with red swirls spinning—entranced by the wicked Mojo.

"Nice animals…" she cooed, backing up. Daring's dream from the inn rushed back to her—the horde of baby animals crying out to her, begging for help. These were the stolen pets of the Tricorner Villages! And she had to find a way to save them, too.

"Stop!" Daring commanded, leaping to her feet. "Stay back! I mean it, you rascals!" She cracked her leather lasso at the horde, creating the space of several hooves between them. "I know you all aren't really like this!" she continued. "Mojo did this to you, didn't he?!" The pets fell silent and stopped dead in their tracks. A few puppies cocked their heads to the side in confusion. An orange kitten perched on a stalagmite began purring.

"I can free you if you lead me to him." Daring knelt down to a large white rabbit with brown spots all over his fur. "Fluffy Bun, I take it?" At this, a blue-colored smoke enveloped him, and when it disappeared, the red glaze drained from his beady eyes. He blinked a few times and looked around at the underground prison as if he was coming out of a dream. Fluffy Bun turned back to Daring Do and nodded. "Bruno? Denise!" Daring called out, recalling the names she'd heard in the village.

A basset hound and a gigantic white goose emerged from the pack. Yellow and red smoke covered them, and the glaze faded from their eyes just as Fluffy's had. The bunny, dog, and bird stood before Daring, now eager to please her.

"Welcome back! Now hurry up and get the others to help, too!" Daring said, pulling out some rope. "I have an idea. But first, I'm going to need you to tie me up."

CHAPTER 12
The Belly of the Beast

The two other prisoners, Golden Rule and Tater Tot, were already in the cage when Daring arrived in the belly of Mojo's volcanic lair. She craned her neck to try to see if the locks would be easy to destroy. But it was too difficult to assess from the position she was in. Her legs and wings were bound with ropes, and she was being pulled along on a cart by twelve possessed puppies and a large bunny who was pretending to be possessed. It was an unusual plan, but Daring trusted her instincts enough to know it had a chance of success. Either way, it had gotten her to Mojo and the others.

"Daring!" Tater Tot cried out, his voice a mixture of panic and relief.

"Ah, my faithful servants! I see that you have brought me a gift," Mojo smiled in delight. "Treats for everyone later. I have a feeling there will be plenty of bones available then." He locked eyes with Daring Do. She did her best to seem like she was struggling against the ropes. It was all part of the act, and it would only work if Mojo believed it.

"You won't get away with this, Mojo!" Daring shouted. She gritted her teeth and let out a low, animalistic growl.

"Yes, I will." Mojo summoned Fluffy Bun and pointed him toward the cage. "Because it appears I get everything I want." Fluffy Bun hopped over to Daring Do. A pair of sheepdogs trotted over and tore the ropes off the pony with their teeth. Fluffy opened the cage and the dogs threw Daring in. Daring whined convincingly, giving the dogs a sly wink. Tater Tot ran over and hid behind her. Golden Rule looked even grungier than when she'd seen him in the forest. His golden mane was matted, clinging to his head in stringy strands. There was black volcanic ash smudged across his cheeks, and his green velvet cloak was missing. Daring could see that he had a wound across his right hoof, possibly inflicted by Mojo, but she couldn't be sure. After everything she'd learned about Golden Rule from Tater Tot, she knew that he was smart enough to have a plan of some sort. He locked eyes with Daring and gave a tiny nod. So he *was* on her side. Daring wondered what exactly his plan was and whether it would interfere with her own.

"Of course I wanted to steal back all three of the Flankara Relics," Mojo continued, completely oblivious to the silent conversation going on behind the bars of the enclosure. He trotted over to a stone pedestal covered in a black velvet cloak. "And look! The powerful Sword of

Lusitano, the Staff of Ponypeii, and your old friend—the Arrow of Marapore." He reached up, swiping the swathes of fabric off to reveal an ornate metal stand. It had three slots, each filled with an elusive relic.

The silver stallion paced around the glowing trifecta of artifacts. The brilliant light shooting from their tips was almost too bright to behold. It lit up the entire room, which Daring now took in. The blackened volcanic walls were arched and completely smooth—a vast contrast to the passageway Daring had unceremoniously landed in. There were several wooden benches facing the platform that were now filling up with the hundreds of pets that Mojo had stolen from Lusitano,

Ponypeii, Marapore, and possibly other distant places. It was as if they were going to watch some sort of show. *A captive audience.* Daring remembered the words from the encyclopedia. *He's bewitched the animals to take his orders and watch him perform the Vehoovius Hex!*

The only thing that separated the benches from the platform was a pit of bubbling molten lava. The whole space looked very much like the belly of Captain Pony's ship, if it had gone upside down. The sailors called it "keeling over." Hadn't Tater Tot said that long ago, the Stalwart Stallion of Neighples was once a commander in the Royal Navy?

"Mo?" Daring whispered to herself. She thought of Steel Anchor and Sea Storm's

conversation back on the ship. They'd said a pony had "turned." Now she understood what they had meant.

Mojo continued to pace back and forth, his hideous scar of a cutie mark appearing even more terrifying in the ghostly light of the relics. He turned to Daring, the corners of his mouth turned up in a devilish smirk. "And I wanted *you*, Daring Do." He walked closer, trying to crack her stony expression.

"Is that so?" Daring replied, unyielding. Though inside, she was trying to make sense of what he'd confessed. Why would the evil stallion want to lure her there, knowing full well that she had the capabilities to put a stop to his plans? There had to be more.

"Oh yes…" Mojo continued, savoring each word that left his lips. He walked over to a large glass vial that had multicolored smoke swirling around in it. He stared at it as he spoke, mesmerized. "That's why I had my friend Golden Rule here pay you a little visit. Naturally, after I pried all the information about the power of the relics out of him, I was hoping to use him as my witness, my very own 'Golden Pedagogue.' But when he showed me that I had it all wrong—that it had to be a golden *Pegasus* with a cutie mark of a volcano on her flank, naturally I was a bit…upset." Mojo's face morphed into one of rage.

Daring looked to Golden Rule in confusion. Her cutie mark was of a compass rose. Surely, he knew that if he had heard of Daring before. Why had he lied about the fact that it was a volcano? Golden Rule coughed and caught Daring's eye. His wink was so fast that she almost missed it. It was a signal for her to just go with it.

Mojo composed himself and continued on. "Alas, I have a tender heart. The poor little schoolteacher pleaded for his life, and I gave him a way to save it. I told him he had to find me that Pegasus or else"— Mojo motioned to the filthy, defeated pony slumped in the corner—"I won't mention what fate he would have had in store, because lucky for him, whatever he did to get you into my clutches worked. And I have even bigger plans for you, my dear. You're to be my new assistant!" His eyes flashed with wicked delight.

Daring struggled against the bars of the cage. "You won't get away with it, Mojo. And I won't let you hurt those innocent villagers by taking away the only protection they have against a volcano that is minutes away from erupting!"

The cavern rumbled, loosening some wayward rocks from the shiplike stone rafters. They hurtled toward the lava, which churned and bubbled in response. Black smoke rose up and wafted over them. Daring couldn't suppress another fit of coughs.

"Aw, somepony got a bit of a sensitive throat?" Mojo twisted his face into a look of faux concern. "But let's call a little weak Pegasus what it is: *weak*. This was never your game, Do." Mojo sneered. "You might as well give it up now! And Golden

Rule here said you were the bravest in Equestria!" Mojo shot Golden Rule a nasty look. "I have to say I'm *sorely* disappointed."

He trotted over to the cage and brought his face in close. Daring struggled against the cage and let out a low growl. Mojo dramatically tossed back his green-and-black mane and laughed. "But still, since you are the Pegasus that fits the bill, I suppose you'll 'Do.'"

Mojo paced back over to the glass vial and gave it a gentle tap. "Aw, look at my little animal souls! Aren't they pretty? Hundreds of them. Took me forever to collect..." The colored swirls inside began to pick up speed, turning into a miniature tornado. As if the two were connected, a larger tornado of lava spiraled up from the pit, nearing the ceiling of the cavernous room. Mojo watched with glee, the flickering fire visible in his glossy, greedy eyes. "This means Vehoovius is almost ready! Then I can perform my spell and the deed will be done. I will have my cutie mark restored, and I will be more powerful than anypony!"

Mojo lunged for the cage and blasted the gate open with a powerful bolt of magic from his horn. "Now let's see that cutie mark of yours!"

"Daring! Cover your cutie mark!!!" Tater Tot cried out in despair. The colt shielded his eyes as Mojo tore Daring's cloak away from her flank. Daring Do and Mojo both gasped at what they found. Daring Do's cutie mark was gone!

CHAPTER 13
Escape from Mount Vehoovius

"But…but…" Mojo took a step back, dumbfounded by the new development. He grabbed Daring's cloak by the neck, brought her muzzle up to his, and growled. "What have you done, Daring?! This ruins everything!"

The golden Pegasus wished she had an

answer, but for the first time, she was actually nervous. Where *had* her beloved compass, the very essence of her pony identity, gone? Daring Do suddenly felt a whole lot weaker. She looked back at her flank in shock. It had to be some sort of trick of the light, right?

Mojo tore out of the cage and rushed over to the relics, his eyes full of fiery rage. He didn't even notice little Tater Tot slipping out and darting toward the entranced animals. Mojo snatched the Sword of Lusitano from the stand, held it high over his head, and placed it on the ground horizontally. It appeared he was going to try to perform the spell anyway!

Golden Rule gasped. He knew what this truly meant—if Mojo succeeded, the power of the relics would be gone...*forever*. Nothing else would ever be able to protect Marapore, Lusitano, or Ponypeii from Mount Vehoovius again.

Everything was falling apart. Golden Rule dashed over to the distracted Daring Do.

"Daring! I know you don't know me, but you have to trust me. Your cutie mark is still there; *he* just can't see it." Golden Rule gestured to Mojo. "Remember the hide ointment I left for you? It was special; it *hides* your cutie mark. It takes a few days to work, but I was hoping you'd figure it out or at least use it." The golden-maned professor smiled. "And you did." He had done a lot of careful planning to make sure she would be safe if she came to rescue the villages.

"What?" Daring replied, coming back to life. "Well, why didn't you say so sooner, Bucko?! Anything else you want to clue me in on?"

Golden Rule spoke very fast. "I actually am the Golden Pedagogue. I tricked him so I could get you here. I knew it would confuse him and you'd save us. I was under a silencing spell when I visited, but I resisted it enough to leave you some clues...."

"Not to be rude, Professor, but we need to cut this lecture short!" She threw the cloak off and snapped into action. "We have work to do! Come on!"

Across the platform, Mojo had the Staff of Ponypeii in his hooves. He cackled maniacally as he lowered it onto the sword in the proper formation. The walls of the cavern rumbled again, and more debris rained down. The smell of sulfur was becoming stronger. Clouds of black smoke rose from every surface.

"Taaaater!" Daring shouted across the bubbling lake of lava. The red baseball cap actually made him easy to spot amid the smoke. Maybe that kid knew what he was doing after all. "You and GR lead the animals out! I'll take care of the rest! Hurry!" Tater nodded, and Golden Rule rushed off to help.

Now it was time for Daring Do to save some villages.

"MOJO!" Daring hollered over the thunderous volcanic activity. "Hand over the arrow. *Now.*" She proceeded toward him with caution. Negotiations were a delicate matter.

"And why should I do that?" Mojo twirled the arrow in his hooves like a baton. "I'm mere moments away from getting what I want. All I have to do is put this arrow there." He pointed to the pile of relics, which were now pulsating with a strange green light. Something was definitely happening, but Daring Do didn't want to stick around to see what it was. Or to become a molten Pegasus, for that matter.

"I've dealt with Ahuizotl, and I can deal with you!"

Mojo froze. "Whose...name...did... you...SAY?!"

"Ahui—!"

"RRRRRRAW!" Mojo dropped the arrow and lunged toward Daring Do. "Don't you know who made me this way?"

"Ahuizotl did this to you?" Daring replied in awe. "But why?" Daring Do knew the doglike monster was evil. He was her *nemesis*, even. But she never expected him to be the answer to this riddle.

"He scarred me!" Mojo lamented. "All because I tried to leave his clan of henchponies. I didn't want to live that life anymore! I wanted to go back to the Navy. Back to my ship with Captain Pony!" He growled, the sound low and guttural.

"You can still fix this!" Daring shouted, wiping away sweat from her forehead. A geyser of lava shot up and almost reached the top of the cave. A considerable drop landed near the relics and sizzled on the hot stone. "You don't have to hurt anypony else. Just give me the relics!"

Mojo looked back at the relics and then to the crumbling cave. He knew that she was right. This was over. He might as well go down with this volcano, as a sea captain would with his ship. That much, he remembered. He looked back at Daring Do. "Take them," he growled. Daring took a small step forward, unsure. "I said, TAKE THEEEEEEM! Get out of here! Leave me!"

The Pegasus zoomed forward and snatched the three relics with one swift motion. She grabbed Mojo's leather quiver and threw them into it. She hovered in the air for a moment, then swooped back down for the glass vial as well. She soared off through the black smoke and out the top of the volcano. She didn't let herself look back at the poor beast she was leaving behind. It was too tragic.

When she had put enough distance between herself and the volcano and could finally breathe again in the delicious fresh air, Daring Do looked back. Smoke billowed from the top of the roaring monster. It looked surreal against the lush tropical backdrop. If the aftermath of its impending doom weren't going to be so sinister, it would have been pretty. But there was only a matter of minutes before Mount Vehoovius was going to explode for real. She knew what she had to do. Three villages. Three relics. One Pegasus. It was worth a shot.

✦ ✦ ✦

Her heart was beating almost as fast as she had flown, but Daring Do had successfully reinstalled the Sword of Lusitano in its rightful place. The statue of a beautiful and powerful mare wasn't hard to find— it was right in the center of town, like in Marapore. And though she hadn't had time to explain how she'd retrieved their precious sword, she could hear the villagers cheering with gratitude as she zipped off toward Ponypeii to do the same.

As she slid the Staff of Ponypeii into the hooves of a stone pony who looked

like an old magician, a group' of uni-
formed ponies galloped by. One of them
was calling out orders like it was some
sort of rescue party. "You ponies take the
groups on the left; I'll go to the right.
Gather everypony up and usher them to
the coast!"

"Captain Pony? Is that you?" Daring
Do couldn't believe it. The famous sea
captain she'd just spent weeks with was
here with his crew! Right now.

The bearded captain stopped in his
tracks. "Do I know you, madam?"

"Of course you do, I—" Daring suddenly remembered the whole "stowing
away" thing. "I think we met once in Trot-
terdam at the port. Anyway, really have
to fly!"

She soared into the great blue and off to her new home village of Marapore. A loud crash came from the mountain. The volcano was starting to flow! The red geyser shot up into the air in powerful spurts, landing against the mountain's sides and heading straight for the villages. Daring Do clenched her teeth and picked up even more speed. That lava wouldn't reach them. Not under *her* watch.

When she saw the town square of Marapore come into sight, she didn't know what to expect. But there everypony was, waiting calmly. Golden Rule and Tater Tot had made it home and were surrounded by the hundreds of pets that still needed to find their ponies. There was a clear path to the statue. Daring Do didn't even bother to land. She flew straight for the stone stallion and slammed the arrow into its hoof in midair. The moment the arrow touched the stone, the relic lit up and two beams of light shot across the town, creating a perfect sixty-degree angle and one corner of a very special triangle.

"The relic has connected with its brothers!" Kaaxtik shouted. "Miss Ravenhoof! You did it! We're protected from the fiery beast!"

At this, Mount Vehoovius expelled another great spray of lava. It was the biggest yet. Multitudes of molten hot liquid rained down through the atmosphere. Everypony crouched in fear. But whenever it got close to the town, there was an invisible force field covering the village. Not a single drop landed on them or their structures. The ponies watched in wonder. It was a miracle. Now there was just one pony left to save.

CHAPTER 14

The Stalwart Stallion of Neighples

It wasn't difficult to find the cave of monkeys a second time. Daring arrived in a matter of minutes. He was there, just as she'd expected, covered in ash and crouched in a corner. A howler monkey was perched near him, staring, unaware of what to make of the whole situation.

Daring couldn't admit she felt so different, but she wanted to try.

"Mojo?" She folded her wings in and walked slowly over to the fallen villain.

He lifted his head, took one look at her, and grunted. "What do you want now?"

"I came to give you something back," she replied. "Your life. And after all you've done to endanger these civilians, you should be grateful for it."

Mojo grimaced. "How do you propose to do that?"

"Captain Pony is in the village of Ponypeii as we stand here. Go to him and tell him you want to rejoin the crew. Take this." She tossed him the glass vial with the swirling colors inside. "On your travels, you must return the spirits to the animals and return the animals to their rightful owners. When you have finished this task, I will take you to where you can be truly healed."

Daring Do wasn't totally bluffing. She knew that it would take Mojo a much longer time to do what she said than for her to find the all-healing Crystal Sphere of Khumn.

Mojo held the vial in his hooves, and a tear came to his eyes. "But why? Why would you do this for me?"

"Because everypony deserves their cutie mark," Daring Do answered. "And I *really* hate Ahuizotl."

CHAPTER 15
Off to the Next Adventure

"What's this?" Daring Do held a brown paper package in her hooves. She was about to depart from Marapore and head back to her cottage for a long, well-deserved breather. The merriment of the villagers' victory against the volcano and the safe return of their pets had finally died down. Daring had drunk her weight in cider and had her fill of mango and pineapple pie. It was always best to leave on a high note such as this. Tater Tot rolled forward on his front hooves excitedly and Golden Rule stood behind him, smirking. "It's a thank-you gift. For everything."

"I don't know if you caught this, but I'm not really a sentimental type..." Daring said as she tore off the wrapping. Daring's jaw dropped. "...except when it comes to books!" It was a one-of-a-kind, hoofwritten text called *Indigenous Magical Plants of the North and South, Volume 5: Flowers.* Gorgeous illustrations of the hibiscus and somnambular blooms in the Maraporian style embellished the cover, and the pages were annotated with Golden Rule's personal research.

"Are you sure you want to part with this, Bucko?" Daring scoffed. "I mean, I already have your encyclopedia back home."

"Believe me, you're going to need it." Golden Rule smiled in a way that made Daring Do wonder. *How* did *he know all this stuff anyway?*

"Well, if you insist." Daring shrugged with a smirk and slid the book safely into her satchel. She leaned down and patted Tater Tot on the head. "Stay outta trouble, all right, kid?" The pipsqueak nodded with a sad smile.

"Don't count on it," he said. She smiled back, tipped her pith helmet, and headed off on her next quest: a relaxed reading session with some dandelion tea in her favorite green armchair.

"Oh, and, Daring?" Golden Rule shouted after her. "*Do* study hard. Particularly something of interest in Chapter Eleven. It's called the Eternal Flower."

Maybe that rest wouldn't be so long after all.

THE END

A. K. Yearling's adventure novels starring the fearless Daring Do have been recognized as the bestselling series in Equestrian history. Yearling holds a degree in literature from Pranceton University. After college, she briefly worked as a researcher at the National Archives for Equestrian Artifacts and Ponthropology in Canterlot. During that time, she wrote an essay based on her findings of the griffon territories, entitled "What Was the Name of That Griffon Again? Or, Beak and Roaming Studies Recalled." It was published by the University of Equexeter's journal, *Pegasus*, last year. She enjoys quiet time alone at home and long trots on the beach.

G. M. Berrow loves to explore exotic locales around the globe, through both the stories she writes and her escapades in real life. Berrow is overjoyed to have collaborated on these adventures with her very own golden idol—A. K. Yearling herself! She adores shiny things, but she thinks the best treasure of all is a book.

GLOSSARY

Ahuizotl (Ow-whee-ZOH-tul): A giant, evil beast who will stop at nothing to gain riches and power. He is Daring Do's biggest foe.

Blood-Eyed Howler Monkey: A vicious breed of monkey with red eyes and long, shiny fur. Indigenous to the jungles and caves of southern Equestria.

Captain Pony the Elder: Captain of the SS *Blue Peter*, a Royal Navy ship.

Crystal Sphere of Khumn (KOOM): A relic theorized to be hidden in one of the Submerged Temples of Tehuti (tay-HOO-tee), located one hundred fathoms below the ocean's surface. It is supposedly held by a statue between two golden hooves, beneath a shining metal rod. The Sphere has the power to heal anypony who touches it, no matter the ailment.

Dr. Caballeron (Cab-uh-LAIR-on): A
rival treasure-hunting pony. Ever since Daring Do refused to work with him as partners, he's made his bits by doing Ahuizotl's dirty work.

Flankara (FLANK-ah-rah) Relics:
Consisting of a staff, a sword, and an arrow, the relics are known to provide the most powerful protection in the world when in close proximity with one another. They serve as protection for the Tricorner Villages against the active volcano Vehoovius.

Forgotten Palace of Tlatelolco
(ta-la-TAY-lohl-co): Ruins near the Tenochtitlan (teen-OACH-teet-lahn) Basin, where Daring Do discovered a room stacked high with ancient gold coins.

Get On Inn: A barn-and-breakfast run by Mrs. Trotsworth and frequented by travelers heading toward the Southern Region of Equestria.

Golden Rule: The schoolteacher in the village of Marapore.

Ketztwctl (kehtz-toh-WEK-tuhl) Empress: An evil ruler who once controlled the Tenochtitlan Basin with the Amulet of Atonement. Daring Do used the Radiant Shield of Razdon (RAZ-dawn) to dispel her dark enchantments and block Ahuizotl's attempt at gaining control over the area.

Mount Vehoovius (vuh-HOO-vee-us): An active volcano surrounded by the villages of Marapore (MAIR-uh-pour), Lusitano (loo-sih-TAHN-oh), and Ponypeii (POH-nee-pay).

Rings of Scorchero (skor-CHAIR-oh): A set of four golden rings that are cursed with a dark enchantment. Prophecy foretells that once the rings are joined together, the valley will be doomed to eight centuries of unrelenting heat. The rings are vulnerable to the Radiant Shield of Razdon.

Sapphire Statue: A two-headed blue stone statue that Daring Do once retrieved from a hidden temple.

Somnambular (som-NAM-bew-ler) Bloom: Large tropical flowers with fuchsia petals and orange stems. These dangerous blooms are known to lull ponies to sleep with their strong perfume, though some varieties affect the pony by making him or her sleepwalk. Commonly found in the southern regions and several tropical isles off the western coast of Equestria.

Tricorner Villages: The three remote villages located at the base of Mount Vehoovius—Marapore, Lusitano, and Ponypeii. The villages work together and exchange goods that are unique to each.

Vehoovius Hex: The Flankara Relics can be arranged in a six-pointed star formation, allowing the possessor to undo any magically inflicted injury. It can only be used once, and legend says it must be witnessed by a captive audience and a "Golden Pedagogue."

Wandering Tree: A magical type of tree that replants itself in different areas at will.

Xihuitl (SHE-wheat-uhl) Grass: Turquoise grass that grows in Marapore.

AS DARING DO SAYS:

"Another adventure awaits..."

Use these pages to record your own brave quests
seeking treasure and to sketch any interesting
flora or fauna you find along the way!

FIELD NOTES

SKETCHES

FIELD NOTES

SKETCHES

FIELD NOTES

SKETCHES

FIELD NOTES

SKETCHES

FIELD NOTES

SKETCHES